Thank you to Vanessa Jensen whose right and left brains saved the day so many times in so many ways and my critique group: Rebecca Bush, Tara Chang, Suzy Cyr, Isobel Davis, Jo Gershman, Kathleen Kemly and Michelle Waldele-Dick for their encouragement and expertise.

And to my husband Jim, daughters Mara, Lissa and Carly, and neighbor Amy for their unflagging support; and my mother, Solveig Geibel, for her imagination and her courage.

Sleep Pony Dreams

Gudrun Geibel Ongman

MindCastle Books, Inc.

If we could see with our hearts,
we would see them,
these little ponies who wait.
But do not be too sad for their waiting.
For long before we learn to call them,
we ride together in their dreams.

Everywhere
Whicker went,
for as long as
she could remember,
wishes to see
her Dream Child
echoed all around her.

"She will kiss your nose," swished the spring grass.
"You will snuggle close," rustled the summer shade trees.
"You will laugh and play," crackled the fall leaves.

And after every wishing from spring through fall
came too many questions with too few answers.

"Why can't I see her today?" pouted Whicker.
"What's so special about Mountain?
Do we have to wait until winter for the Gathering?
What is 'whinn-ter' anyway?"

Whicker knew Grandmare's answers by heart
long before she understood them.
"Before the Gathering of the herds, come the spring birthings
and summer growings, then the fall storings and winter sleepings.
Mountain will not be ready for us to climb
until geese have waved goodbye and branches bow to snow."

Whinny answered
Whicker's questions with lists
of every kind of growing.

"You must snuggle like a baby bunny
and love like a daddy fox,
listen like a fawn and tease like a jay,
then plan like a squirrel for winter
and play like the baby horse you are."
And so Whicker practiced and played
until there was just one more thing to learn . . .

. . .the patience of a bird on eggs.

Try as she might to remember the soft and still of Mommy Robin on her fragile,
sky-blue eggs, Whicker could not stop tossing her head and pawing
the ground as she listened to the endless answers of her herd,
"Someday . . . . in a while . . . . not today."

When she was especially tired and discouraged,
when she thought the Gathering would never come,
Whinny's child would hug her and kiss her velvet nose
until hope returned . . .

and the wishing grew stronger.

One day Whicker's wishing
took the form of a snowflake.
Before long millions of tiny hushed voices
were whispering . . . *"S-o-o-o-o-o-n-n-n!"*

"Grandmare, let's go now!
PLEASE, can we go now?"
"Remember the robin,"
Grandmare cautioned.

So Whicker
measured the snow
from first flake
to mouse-deep.
And as she helped friends carry food,
crack ice and reach the highest berries,
time passed more quickly.

One morning she awoke to see the snow was
finally thick enough. The hush of falling snow
mingled distant neighs with soft goodbyes.

"Our best to your cousin Shimmer
and the other foals," yawned Raccoon.
"And to your Dream Child,"
waved Robin on her way south.

"Come Whicker," Grandmare called, "It's time.
We must reach Mountain's meadow before dark
or you will miss your Dream Child!"

So Whicker whirled
and charged up the hill ahead of her herd,
and the sun began its path across the sky.

On that long,
cheerful journey, through all the
rompings and runnings

and greetings and meetings,
through all the games and contests
and tricks and teasings,

every Sleep Pony Whicker met
kept moving up the mountain,
matching its pace to the sun.

Most of the herds reached
Mountain's meadow in time
to relax and play, and then to watch
the late afternoon sun
light the frozen waterfall
and hear its icicles whisper . . .

"S-s-o-o-o-o-o-o-n!"

But life does not always travel steady like the sun.
Very late that afternoon,
Whicker's uncle raced alone
and steaming into camp.

"We cannot come tonight,
little Shimmer is just too tired
to finish the climb."

"And miss his
Dream Child?"
Whicker gasped.
"Not if I can help it!"

"Can we come too?"
asked her friend.

"We'll make it back," Whicker called.

"We'll make it back in time," she hoped
as she glanced toward the sun.

Some say the sun heard and
slowed enough for hope to race ahead.

Some say hooves never touched the snow.

But all who watched
were certain of Whicker's courage
and of the warmth that filled her
when she found Shimmer
asleep, yet somehow waiting.

All saw that warmth
strengthen Whicker as she helped
support her little cousin, step by step, upward,
their shadows lengthening in the setting sun.

And all felt the warmth themselves

as Whicker led Shimmer
into the meadow, the sun slipped
below the horizon
and the celebration began.

By moonlight, foals snuggled close to grandmares
to watch dancers leap and bow.
Wherever warm bodies met the cold that night, a mist was born.
And when the mist was nearly ready, it whispered . . .

"S-o-o-o-o-o-o-o-n!"

Then
dancers came
with secret smiles
to say goodnight,

and as they carried
their children home,

the mist grew with them.

When its path stretched from Icicle Falls to the furthest valleys below,
grandmares nudged their grandfoals forward.

"*N-n-n-o-o-o-o-o-w-w-w!*" breathed the mist
and as it shortened to the length of a whisker . . .

. . . Whicker saw her child, and forgot all else.

"When you are ready," she promised silently,
"I will show you how to stay warm in winter,
how Fish swims below the ice
and Otter slides above.
Together, we will say goodnight
to the day and snuggle close.
You will hold my mane with
hands and ribs with knees,
laugh our love and
hug me tight,

and I will carry you far and fast,
and you will not be afraid.
I will be there whenever you call . . .

. . . and also when you don't."

All through that long night
and the many to follow,
Whicker dreamed about these things.

And though the wind blew and the temperature dropped,
she slept cozy warm for she could see her Dream Child . . .

. . . and had learned the robin's secret.

And somewhere far away
yet very close,
like children all over the world,
a little girl pushed back her covers
for she was suddenly very warm.

To Susan Mossey and that part of everyone
that love feeds and beauty inspires.

May it carry you far.

G.G.O.

First Edition
Published by MindCastle Books, Inc.
P.O. Box 3005
Woodinville, WA 98072
www.mindcastle.com
MindCastle is a registered trademark of MindCastle Books, Inc.

The text is set in Adobe Garamond Pro
Printed on Acid Free, Recyclable Paper
Illustrations are rendered in watercolor and pastel
Designer: Vanessa Jensen

Library of Congress Cataloging in Publication Data

Ongman, Gudrun Geibel
Sleep pony dreams/Gudrun Geibel Ongman - 1-st ed.
p.cm
SUMMARY: A young sleep pony climbs a mountain to attend a winter Sleep Pony
celebration and learns the lessons that enable her to see her Dream Child.

Library of Congress Control Number: 2005931721

ISBN: 978-0-9677204-2-5

[1. Horses-Juvenile fiction, 2. Dreams-Juvenile fiction,
3. Winter-Juvenile fiction, 4. Sleep-Juvenile fiction.]
I. Ongman, Gudrun Geibel. II. Title.

Printed in Korea

10 9 8 7 6 5 4 3 2 1